To our biggest loves, Poppy and Daisyboo,
and to all the little girls and boys we know – J. O.

To Peter and Alice, Joyce and Malcolm,
and with thanks to Saffron, Matilda and Adam – C. F.

PUFFIN BOOKS
Published by the Penguin Group: London, New York, Australia,
Canada, India, Ireland, New Zealand and South Africa
Penguin Books Ltd, Registered Offices: 80 Strand, London WC2R 0RL, England

puffinbooks.com

First published 2008
1 3 5 7 9 10 8 6 4 2
Text copyright © Jools Oliver, 2008
Illustrations copyright © Claire Fletcher, 2008
Printed in China
ISBN: 978–0–141–38377–4

The Adventures of
Dotty and Bluebell

4 delightful stories of an Ever-So-Naughty Little Girl and her Big Sister

JOOLS OLIVER
Illustrated by CLAIRE FLETCHER

PUFFIN

Dotty

Bluebell

Jake

Not so very long ago and not so very far from your house lived three best friends – well, two sisters and a little boy next door. Their names were **Dotty**, **Bluebell** and **Jake**.

Dotty was three years, nine months and five days old. Bluebell, her older sister, was four years, eleven months and twelve days old. And Jake was six. They all went to the same school just up the lane and round the corner from their houses.

Now, the two little girls had lived in the same village and the same house for all their lives with their mummy and daddy and their two rabbits called Poppy-Loppy and Ben. On the other hand, Jake had only moved in next door about three and a half weeks ago. He arrived with his guinea pig Sweety, and a handful of other strange creatures, each in their own home. There was a lizard in a jam jar, a spider in a cardboard box decorated with rainbows on the side and a little matchbox with three ladybirds. The matchbox had holes in the top. "Of course," Jake reliably informed the girls, "this is to keep the ladybirds from suffocating."

Jake, you see, knew lots about everything, and Bluebell, being the eldest sister, was a sensible sort of girl. As for Dotty, well, sometimes she could be very naughty and that meant the best plans of all often went very, very wrong.

Spring

Once upon a bright spring morning, the three best friends were up and dressed very early. They were going to visit a farm because it was the first day of spring.

"Do you think there will be yellow chicks and rabbits with flopsy ears?" asked Dotty. Dotty always spoke quickly when she was excited. "And-will-there-be-ice-cream-in-a-cone-because-that-is-my-favourite?"

"There will be ALL SORTS of things," said Jake. "We can feed the baby chicks and watch the cows being milked and, if we're VERY lucky, we might see some newborn lambs."

"I love lambs!" said Bluebell. "They are my most favourite animal of all."

But Dotty was especially happy because Jake had mentioned chicks. She had always wanted a little yellow chick. *I will call it Fluffball*, she thought, *and it will live with Poppy-Loppy and Ben in their rabbit house. Oooohhh-this-is-going-to-be-a-brilliant-day.*

So when the grown-ups were finally ready they all set off. Jake's pockets were bulging with matchboxes and jam jars, Dotty wore her pink fairy wings, and Bluebell (who liked to be well prepared) had brought raincoats, wellies and snacks.

Well, what a day it was! First of all, Dotty, Bluebell and Jake had a ride on a tractor.

"This is a very special tractor," said Jake. "It's called Speedy."

But, in fact, it was a bit slow and bumpy, which made them all laugh. Then they stopped to watch the cows being milked.

"Just think!" said Bluebell. "This is where the milk comes from for our breakfast every morning."

The cows all had different names and the children took it in turns to stroke their velvety noses.

But Dotty said, "Where's the chocolate cow that makes the chocolate milk? Look, all the cows are white."

"Silly," said Jake. "Chocolate milk is made when you mix white milk with special chocolate powder."

Next to the cows was a place called the lambing shed.

"This is where all the little lambs are born," explained the farm lady.

Some of the mummy sheep were very big and Bluebell wondered if they might be having two babies.

"But WHY are there so many baby animals?" asked Dotty. "Do they ALL have mummies?"

"Of course they do," said the farm lady. "Spring is when lots of animals have their babies, when the weather gets warmer and daffodils start to grow."

"Oh," piped up Bluebell. "I know that because that's when me and Dotty were born. In the springtime, Mummy said."

Last of all, they went to see the baby chicks. Dotty was so excited that she hopped on one foot, then on the other. They each took it in turns to cuddle and stroke the fluffy chicks and Jake said that this was the best thing of all. Dotty was very quiet and gently stroked the warm bundles of fluff against her cheek. It really had been a very brilliant day.

It was quite late, at least three o'clock, when it was time to go home. Jake went to Bluebell and Dotty's house for tea and they all had cake, which was a special spring cake with chocolate eggs on top. They were about to have a story when Dotty said, "I have an earache now and I would like to go to bed with no bath, and can-I-go-by-myself-can-I-please?"

Now, this was very surprising indeed. Dotty NEVER went to bed early and she NEVER missed storytime. Bluebell and Jake were extremely curious. Just as soon as they could, they both raced upstairs.

an you guess what that naughty little Dotty had done? There, next to Blue Rabbit and Spotty Dog, was a very yellow, very fluffy chick.

"Dotty!" said Bluebell. "That's a chick from the farm!"

"No. No, it isn't," said Dotty crossly. "As-a-matter-of-fact, I found her in my bed. Her name's Fluffball."

"But, Dotty, that's not true. Mummy and Daddy will be ever so angry!" said Bluebell.

And at that, Dotty began to cry. "I just popped her in my pocket," she sobbed. "There were so many babies and not nearly enough mummies. And I so wanted a fluffy chick!"

"There, there," said Bluebell. "But we will have to take her back. She will miss her mummy AND she will be ever so hungry."

"Jake can help," said Dotty. "You know about chicks, don't you, Jake? And I will be the Best Mummy Ever because I've been practising."

"Actually, I do know about chicks," said Jake importantly. "They like worms."

"See?" said Dotty. "Fluffball will be ever so happy."

And that was that. Jake went to look for worms, and Bluebell and Dotty decided that they would all look after the chick in turn: Dotty first, then Bluebell, then Jake. It was all very exciting, but not for Bluebell. She hated being naughty.

That night, Dotty, Blue Rabbit, Spotty Dog and Fluffball all went to sleep in Dotty's bed (although Fluffball had her very own bed in a cardboard box). It was all quiet, apart from an occasional cheep.

But then, when it was dark in the very middle of the night, Fluffball went for a little walk. And can you guess where she went? Yes, that's right– MUMMY AND DADDY'S BED!

Well, what a noise! Mummy jumped out of bed in fright and Daddy gave a great big yell, which, of course, woke up Bluebell and Dotty.

Everyone was wide awake, and all because of a little chick.

"Fluffy!" cried Dotty. "I love you!"

But Bluebell started to cry. "We didn't mean to be naughty," she sobbed and Daddy had to give her a big cuddle.

As you can imagine, there was a great deal of explaining to do. Dotty sat on Mummy's lap and told the whole story from the very beginning to the very end. And when she had told them everything, she said, "I'm-ever-so-very-sorry-Mummy. I-won't-do-it-again."

After a gentle telling-off, Mummy and Daddy decided that the best thing to do was to take the little chick back to the farm. "After all," said Mummy. "Fluffball is only a baby and she must be homesick."

Mummy was quite right. *ALL babies, big and small, need their mummies*, thought Dotty.

So the very next morning, Dotty, Bluebell, Mummy AND Fluffball drove back to the farm. Fluffball cheeped all the way, but Dotty was quiet. She would miss her new friend.

But something surprising happened. Once the girls had explained to the farm lady how sorry they were, the farm lady (who was a little bit cross, but not very) asked if they would like to officially name the chick "Fluffball". And, what's more, she said Dotty and Bluebell could visit whenever they liked!

"Can Jake come too?" asked Bluebell.

"Oh-yes-please!" said Dotty.

And Mummy said, "But only if you promise to behave."

"We promise!" said the girls together.

And that was the end of that.

Summer

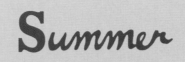

When Dotty woke up, she just knew something was different. She leapt out of bed and rushed into Bluebell's room.

 t's here," she cried, "it's here!" And she jumped up and down on Bluebell's bed. "Wake up, sleepy-head. Summer's here!"

Dotty was right. The birds were singing, the leaves were fat and emerald green, the sun was high and bright – yes, it was a perfect summer's day.

Dotty then raced into Mummy and Daddy's room and started to bounce on THEIR bed. In between each bounce, she shouted, "WE LOVE SUMMER! WE LOVE SUMMER!" until finally Daddy said, "Right, grab your buckets and spades – we're off to the beach!"

Now, this was very exciting indeed. The beach, you see, was Dotty's most favourite place because Nanny and Grandpa lived there. They owned a little house near the sea, and whenever Bluebell and Dotty visited, they would always have a campfire and sometimes there would be fireworks too.

"Hooray!" shouted Dotty happily. "We're going to have an ADVENTURE!"

Naturally, Jake came too, and all the way in the car, the children made plans.

"I'm going to build a sandcastle for a princess," said Bluebell, "with turrets and flags and pretty shells."

"I want to look for crabs," said Jake. "And anemones and starfish. But I want to find a crab the most, I think."

Dotty, who had brought ALL her favourite toys, said, "I-want-to-paddle-all-the-way-up-to-my-toes, but NO MORE in case Blue Rabbit and Spotty Dog get scared." Dotty loved the seaside, but she didn't like the way the waves chased her up the beach.

They were VERY hot by the time they arrived, so Dotty, Bluebell and Jake ran straight down to the sea. Bluebell and Jake went in right up to their knees, but Dotty stayed at the edge. She dipped her toe in now and again, explaining carefully that Blue Rabbit was a bit scared.

Soon it was time to eat the special picnic Nanny and Grandpa had brought, and then it was on to the sandcastle competition.

"Mine is the biggest!" said Dotty proudly.

"But mine is the prettiest," said Bluebell. Dotty scowled, but Bluebell was quite right. HER castle had eight turrets, a moat, white shells AND pink flags.

Jake, of course, was busy looking for crabs. "This is the very best one!" he said. "It's a hermit crab, which is just like a snail because he carries his home on his back."

Grandpa then said it was time for a swim. He scooped up Bluebell and dashed into the sea. Dotty, however, just wanted to sit with Blue Rabbit and Spotty Dog and watch the little waves rush in and then back out again. They didn't seem so scary really, and she liked the whoosh-swoosh noise they made. And then Blue Rabbit whispered something in Dotty's ear . . .

Well, you'll never guess what Dotty did next. She pulled the little dinghy down to the water and placed Blue Rabbit and Spotty Dog inside. Just like that! Now, both you and I know that this wasn't a very sensible thing to do, but Dotty wasn't always the most sensible girl. She pushed the dinghy out and watched excitedly as the boat rose up and down on the little waves.

"Isn't this fun!" she cried.

But then a big wave came in. And another one, and instead of bobbing back to shore, the little boat began to sail away. "Come back!" called Dotty. "Come-back-now!" But Blue Rabbit and Spotty Dog were too far away to hear.

Naturally, Dotty burst into tears and Mummy and Daddy came rushing over.

"Whatever's wrong?" they asked.

"We were just playing," sobbed Dotty, pointing at the boat, "but now it's gone wrong, and I think Spotty Dog is seasick!"

Luckily, the boat hadn't gone very far at all. Daddy waded out and pulled the dinghy back in, and, of course, Blue Rabbit and Spotty Dog were just fine. "That wasn't a very clever thing to do," Daddy then said. "You must be careful when playing by the sea."

Dotty hiccupped a bit and said it had been a VERY good adventure, but she didn't mean to be naughty (even though it had all been Blue Rabbit's idea).

anny said it was definitely time for tea now and that there had been quite enough excitement for one day.

"Can I help build the campfire?" asked Jake.

"And can I cook the sausages?" said Bluebell.

Dotty just sat on Grandpa's knee with Spotty Dog and Blue Rabbit, and they soon had the most delicious tea. After a little while, Dotty whispered in Grandpa's ear, "Actually, Grandpa, Blue Rabbit and Spotty Dog DO like the sea. And-I-think-maybe-I-do-too."

The sun began to set and lots of people, big and small, began to gather on the beach. Then, with all the children tucked in blankets, the clear sky suddenly filled with fireworks and everyone agreed that summer really had begun.

Autumn

Dotty was NOT happy.
Bluebell said she was too
busy to play, Spotty Dog
was in the washing machine
AND it was pouring with rain.

Dotty scowled. She hated the rain. *What a back-to-front, upside-down day,* she thought. She stared out of the window gloomily and then stomped downstairs.

Dotty was so busy being miserable that she bumped right into Jake.

"It's not fair," she said. "It's not a day for adventures AT ALL!"

"Silly," said Jake. "Yes, it is. Did you forget that it's our Halloween party tomorrow? I'm going to be a cowboy wizard with a cowboy hat AND a magic cloak."

"And that's why I was busy," said Bluebell, who had two black ears in her hair. "I'm a witch's cat, only I don't know how to make a tail."

Well, of course, Dotty HAD forgotten all about Halloween. "A party!" she gasped. "Oooohh-I-can't-wait." Naturally, Dotty knew what she wanted to be right away. "I'm going to be a fairy witch," she said, "with a pink tutu, pink wellies AND a special pink wand."

Very soon, the three best friends settled down to make plans. First, they decided, they would have a scary tea, then play skeleton games in the garden and then have the very special spider cake Mummy had baked. It had eight legs, a chocolate body and pink marshmallows for eyes.

By the time it was bedtime, Dotty was so excited she couldn't sleep. Halloween wasn't quite as exciting as Christmas, she thought. Or her birthday, but it was still A LOT of fun and just like an adventure.

he very next day, the children rushed home from school and changed into their Halloween costumes. Just as they had planned, they had a VERY scary tea. There were Marmite sandwiches in the shape of bats, fairy cakes with black butterflies on top, sticky toffee apples and mountains of juicy blackberries.

Dotty, however, wanted to know when they were going to eat the spider cake. "I have waited soooo long," she said.

"But you have to wait some more," said Bluebell, "until Mummy says. Come on, let's go and play!"

All the children had been growing vegetables and had grown the biggest pumpkin they had ever seen. Jake, being the eldest, was allowed to use a knife and cut out a face with a big toothy grin. Then, once they had lit the pumpkin, it was time for the skeleton game. Daddy had hidden paper skeletons with little treats all over the garden.

"Ooohhh," said Dotty, who loved playing games. "Isn't-this-exciting?"

Jake found the first skeleton and a bag of chocolate buttons, and then Bluebell found another one in Daddy's shed. All the time, there were scary noises that made them jump. Now, you and I know that it was probably Daddy hiding and making silly sounds, or maybe it was a little fox, but Jake, Bluebell and Dotty didn't know, and they were scared to their very bones.

In fact, Dotty was a bit TOO scared. Even though Blue Rabbit was with her, the dark seemed big and frightening. "Come on, Blue Rabbit," she whispered. "Let's go inside."

They went into the kitchen, but as soon as Dotty saw the chocolate spider cake, an idea popped into her head. The cake was exactly the right size for a toys' tea party. Dotty picked it up and rushed upstairs.

Now, you and I know this wasn't a very good idea, but not Dotty. Very soon, she had everything for a perfect tea party, but where was Spotty Dog? "I can't have a party without Spotty Dog," she said, and began to search her room. She was just reaching up to look behind her storybooks, when her foot slipped . . .

BUMP! SMACK! Dotty fell off the bed and landed right on the chocolate spider cake.

Well, there was chocolate everywhere! It was all over Blue Rabbit, all over Oscar the cat AND all over Dotty's pink tutu. Dotty began to cry.

Outside, it was now VERY dark and everyone was ready for cake. They all trooped inside, but the kitchen table was COMPLETELY EMPTY.

"Where's Dotty?" said Jake.

"I think I know," said Bluebell, hearing a funny noise from upstairs. "Quick, follow me!"

hey both raced upstairs and dashed into Dotty's room. And when they saw Dotty sitting there, in a big puddle of cake with a chocolate smudge on her nose, they both began to laugh.

"Oh, Dotty," said Bluebell. "You do look funny."

"It's not funny," sobbed Dotty. "I couldn't find Spotty Dog. Then-I-fell-on-my-bottom-and-now-the-cake-doesn't-look-like-a-spider-any-more!"

"Don't cry," said Bluebell. "It's just a silly cake. Look, we can put it back together again, just like Humpty Dumpty."

"Here are the marshmallow eyes," said Jake.

"Here's a leg!" said Dotty, starting to giggle.

"And there's another one!" said Bluebell, laughing all over again.

Very soon, the three friends had mended the cake. It didn't really look like a spider any more, but that didn't matter. It was now a very scary monster cake – perfect for Halloween!

When they went back downstairs, Dotty rushed over to Mummy and explained everything. "I'm-ever-so-very-sorry," she said. "I won't do it again."

Mummy made a cross face, but, luckily, she thought it was quite funny too. "Come on," she said. "I think it must be time for a piece of monster cake now!"

Soon everyone had a slice of cake and glass of warm milk.

"I do love Halloween," said Dotty, munching her cake.

"Yes, but now we must make plans for Bonfire Night," said Bluebell.

"We have to have fireworks!" said Jake.

"And a CAKE!" said Dotty, and everyone laughed.

Winter

It was only four days, three hours and seventeen minutes until Christmas Day, and Dotty was VERY excited.

very day she rushed downstairs to open a window on her advent calendar, and every day she counted how many days were left. But it was still a long time to wait and sometimes Dotty felt Christmas would never come. "Please, Father Christmas," she said. "Please hurry up and come RIGHT NOW!"

Luckily, there were lots of things to do to keep busy. At school, there was a special Christmas play of *Jack and the Beanstalk*. Bluebell was the golden egg, Jake was the back end of the cow, and Dotty had a green costume with a green hat because she was a magic bean. Mummy also needed lots of help in the kitchen – it was Dotty and Bluebell's job to measure the raisins and then stir them into the Christmas pudding. So, when Grandpa said that he had a special treat, the children almost burst with excitement.

"Tell us, Grandpa!" cried Dotty. "Tell us now!"

"Is it a tractor ride?" said Jake.

"Is it ice-skating?" said Bluebell.

"No, something much more exciting!" said Grandpa. "We're going to meet Father Christmas!"

Now, this was VERY exciting news indeed. Dotty was so excited that for the first time EVER she didn't know what to say, and Jake just jumped up and down. Bluebell, however, looked worried. "But where does Father Christmas live?" she asked.

"Don't worry," said Jake. "I know where he lives. My grandpa told me he lives in the village, in the garden centre where your daddy buys his tools."

But Dotty suddenly went very quiet. Yesterday Mummy had made her sit on the naughty step because she had eaten some of the chocolate decorations on the Christmas tree. *Oh dear*, she thought. *I hope Father Christmas didn't see. I-do-so-want-a-dancing-ballerina.*

he day of the great event finally arrived. And can you guess what happened? During the night, when Dotty and Bluebell were tucked up and fast asleep, snow had started to fall. When the children woke up, everything was still and perfectly white.

"It's today, Bluebell, it's today!" Dotty cried, as she bounced on the bed. "Today is the day we see Father Christmas in his lotto."

Bluebell, who was still half-asleep, giggled. "No, Dotty, it's not *lotto*, it's *grotto*. It's the special place where Father Christmas makes all the toys!"

Everyone bundled up in scarves and gloves and ran outside to play in the snow. Dotty pretended to be a pink polar bear while Bluebell and Jake built a snowman with a great fat tummy. Then they all had a competition to see who could make the best snow angel. Dotty said that hers was the prettiest, but Jake was really the winner because his was the largest of all.

Grandpa then said it was time to go. Jake, of course, was in front. He was carrying a rucksack for the toy soldiers he hoped Father Christmas would give him, while Bluebell held Grandpa's hand and told him the secret list of what she would like for Christmas. Dotty, as usual, was last. She and Spotty Dog were counting all the Christmas trees and trying to decide which ones they liked best.

At long last they arrived at the garden centre, but it was very busy. Lots of other children wanted to see Father Christmas too, and Dotty was worried he might run out of toys.

"It's not fair," she scowled. "I want to see Father Christmas FIRST! What if there aren't enough toys?"

"Hush," said Bluebell. "Of course there will be enough toys. But Mummy said you have to wait."

"Did you hear that, Spotty Dog?" said Dotty. "We must wait NICELY." So Dotty held on to Bluebell's hand and hopped from one foot to the other until, finally, it was their turn.

Everyone went very quiet. The entrance to the grotto was through a tiny tunnel of trees full of bright, twinkling lights – Dotty thought she had never seen anything so magical in her life. Little elves told them where to go, and there was just enough room for Grandpa to squeeze in too.

They all heard a big, cheery "Ho, ho, ho!" and there, sitting in a big golden chair, was Father Christmas. Everyone was so excited they didn't know what to say.

First of all, Father Christmas asked each of the children what they would like for Christmas. Jake wanted a special bug-catcher to keep ladybirds in, and Bluebell wanted a jewellery box with real jewels and some fairy stickers. Finally, it was Dotty's turn. She reached up and whispered her wish very quietly into Father Christmas's ear.

Father Christmas promised that he would do his best, but in the meantime, all three children had to be very good or they might find a lump of coal in their stockings instead!

You see, the sleigh hadn't been flying at all. Dotty was still at the garden centre and the shop assistants were just putting the sleigh away, ready for Father Christmas and the children tomorrow. Well, you can imagine how surprised everyone was! There, in the middle of all the presents, was a little girl with blonde wavy hair and a spotty toy dog. And when Dotty saw that she was lost and all on her own, she burst into tears.

Jake, Bluebell and Grandpa came rushing over. "Thank goodness you're safe!" cried Grandpa, and they all hugged Dotty so tightly that she didn't have the breath to cry any more.

"We didn't mean to be naughty," she said. "And-I-think-I-would-really-like-to-go-home-now-please."

When they arrived home, Dotty ran straight into her mummy's arms.

"Dotty," said Mummy, "you must never, ever run away again. Mummy and Daddy and Bluebell love you so much and you scared us all."

Dotty sniffed and said that she was very sorry. "It was a very good adventure, but then I got scared and we didn't find the dancing ballerina, did we, Spotty Dog?"

"And, Mummy," said Bluebell, "was it really Father Christmas? And was it really his sleigh? Because there weren't any reindeer."

"Well," Mummy said, "Father Christmas never takes his real sleigh to the grotto because the elves in the North Pole are busy polishing it for Christmas Eve."

"But-was-he-the-real-Father-Christmas-or-not?" asked Dotty.

"Well," said Daddy, "we'll just have to wait and see."

Luckily, there were only a few days to wait. Then, one very cold and snowy morning, Christmas arrived.

Dotty ran into Bluebell's room with her stocking and both girls eagerly unwrapped their presents. There, at the very top, was Dotty's dancing ballerina, but when she got to the bottom of the stocking, she felt something round and hard. It was a dirty piece of black coal.

"Look, Bluebell!" said Dotty. "Father Christmas must have known that I was naughty!"

"And that means he must be real!" said Bluebell.

"I promise that I will never, EVER be naughty again," said Dotty, and the two sisters giggled, knowing very well that naughty little Dotty would find it impossible to keep her promise!